UNDER THE WILD BLUE

Adam Christopher Moorhead

ISBN 978-1-960546-66-1 (paperback)
ISBN 978-1-960546-67-8 (digital)

Rushmore Press LLC
1 800 460 9188
www.rushmorepress.com

Printed in the United States of America

Running on Low

You don't have to tell me…
This world is so cold.
You don't have to sell me…
I hear what I am told.
If it's not about that income
Tell me how I should try to earn some.
Because I am sweating it…
I am feeling it…
I am pressed by it…
I can't seem to get over the hill.
I can't seem to stop worrying about it.
And moving, and moving, and moving…
Fast.

Where I draw the strength
To keep going
Comes from knowing
That I would be wasting my time
Doing what does not bring joy…
And helping a friend or two
Who also might be running on low,
On more than just the cash flow.

So, I promise I won't sell my soul
To anyone's charter or to anyone's voice.
I will keep the opportunity, the choice
To fill up again and to thrive,
Where I might be working at what I love
And what I might do for others
As I seek what comes from above
And what might be heavenly.

Someone, Anyone to Depend On

Another day in, another day out
Burning the clock…
Passing time away…
Like watching an hourglass and the sand that falls.
Another day older
Only slightly though.
Is there anyone to call?
To speak to face to face?
To have a little discussion?
Not about money or numbers
Just about everything else.
No matter how many people know me
Or have known me,
Who is it that truly cares?
Who really wants to stop and sit and listen for a minute?
Or is there no one who truly wants to be depended upon?
To listen, to slow, to chat, to recover, to understand?
Is there anyone to depend on for this?
Or do I need to type it all out for the world to see?
Trust is so fragile these days.
Can trust be found with a human anywhere?
I guess that is where my hope remains:
I believe we can learn to trust
And forgive
And learn to relate with each other.
Not everyone, maybe a few
Who might find the time…
Who knows, it just might be you.

Temporary Rush of a Distraction

A flash, a sound, a movement
Action
Loud
A "head turner"
Beauty
Anything to distract me from this moment.
So easily distracted I am.
But I love it, and I ask for it.
I welcome anything that fills a rush of excitement,
Of worth, of great value or feeling.
Call me soft, name me a pet name,
Whatever.
It's the adrenaline rush that I seek, attention, or to give my attention
To something greater than just the mundane.
Boredom carries with it a disease.
I do not want to pass away from endless fights
With this pandemic.
Have mercy on me, have mercy.

Overcomer

So, I looked you up today.
You might not remember much of me
From so long ago.
And not that we were the best of friends,
But somehow, I heard about your success
In what you do.
We are not the same.
We are so very different.
But nearly two decades of working toward your dream…
And you did it.
You are doing it.
Because you believed,
And because others believed in you.

Not everyone believes, you realize this.
And hearing you speak about the trenches
And the grind, and the tougher days
Over nearly two decades…
Well, I guess I can say: many days feel like the trenches right now…
Yet like you, I still believe.

But here you are
Now
Today
And you did it.
You made it.
Through such dedication
And through toughness
And through tears
And through sweat
And through betrayals.
You are truly an inspiration.

You are the overcomer.

What Music Does, Slowly

Artist. Singer. Creative sound-maker…
I never picked up any of your records.
But I sure listened a lot.
You know how it works these days, with the internet.
I remember your strength, your voice, your words, a piano.
You never toured where I live,
So, I never saw your live show
With exception of what you shared on YouTube.

You took a break from touring.
You rested for a few years.
I picked up your biography book, and you should know.
Though whoever wrote it is not an artist.
And you should know.
I only wanted to hear more music.
But you had nothing further to show.
Your fans were so upset.
And I was one.

I saw your exposure on national TV today.
"Wow" is all I can say.
You must have really worked, and worked, and worked it all out.
You made it back.
After so long.
You seemed so different, so clear, so happier, so healthy…

You have a lot of fans out there, who love your music.
I could be one too,
If you ever play a show down my way.
I will be one regardless, and all I can say
Is nothing but just play. Just play…
You have held my attention
And your story will not remain unwritten.
Have a drink while I write my way into it.

Heavy

Caught a glimpse in the mirror
Wondering if I will ever feel great
Wondering if I could be twenty-one again
In shape, and living it.
But I just feel so heavy, feel it deep, man.

Understanding and seeing eye to eye
Is what I have always wanted
A glimpse beyond the genes, beyond the outside.
Is it all just random and chance?
The chemicals that fire, and the personality inside.

I agree, I can't preach to anyone, about anything.
I tried once, never happened and it left me
Wanting to just hide, man.
Many have just heard it all before.
I guess that's where I come from, asking for a second chance, man.

So, I can't stand up and trim down fast
It would be too tough, and maybe I need to eat less or something
But you have to see and hear beyond what can be seen or heard
It comes off heavy, I know, all this.
But tell me I am being vague, abstract maybe, but never without a word.

Heavy…

Dirty Date

Angel and not a devil…
Not me, no way babe.
Never going to admit that
It was you who kept me rolling through
Those cold days and even colder nights
Humble with no pride…
Not me, no way babe.

When you start calling me by my first name
I know it's not good, babe.
Like a bad note played out of sync
With the rest of everyone else's harmony.
After all, who is really the one to blame here?
Not me, babe.

So, we went out on a date,
Took care of everything babe.
Down to dressing the part and smiling
And even playing the part
And kissed lightly a good kiss goodnight.
That was all, in the end, you stopped talking again.
It all started before we even began, babe.
Just believe we will pass in the streets again,
Maybe around the new year holiday
Or closer to your birthday
Which I forgot already.

The Palace

Let it fly…
Express yourself
Let it fly…
I heard your rhythm and your words
They inspire me to keep moving on
Going on
Typing on
Until I can't sit inside anymore
And I've got to join the club, I've got to go.

I heard too many people saying such hatred
This week, it was beyond entertainment.
I almost felt my ears bleed
But they didn't and I survived
At the Palace
I was there, at the Palace.

You must understand: so many older gents try to teach me
Try to correct me
Try to push me, toward literary perfection.
No such thing, never such a day.

Let it fly…
Express yourself
Let it fly…

No Time for Hate

There is no one who can understand
What it's like to experience hatred
Over race
And skin tone
At least I will never understand the rage.

Some creations from a war,
How many years ago?

What does he mean?
How does he sound?
Stop,
Chill…

I am scared for you,
Only for your hateful mouth,
Your ongoing frustration with your life.
Stay with us, be merciful for a neighbor.

Winner

Friend, if I might say that…
It will be ok
It will all work out
I promise.
Stay with me here, do not walk away.
I know you had your heart set
In the contest, the win.
If I might, we all will love you
Even if you do not win.
I promise.
Stay with me here, do not walk away.

You have been around the world
In the spotlight for so long
Competing, and competing.
We all know your cause.
We all know you.
We hear you; we see you.
If everything was all about winning,
We would not have the contests.
Win or lose, you are (in my eyes)
Great.
I support you; I hear you; I see you.

I stayed near you once
Near where you worked, it was a luxury.
I felt some sort of love…
Like a fathering of sorts.
After my father had departed the world,
Many years earlier, and too early at that.
But it is that fathering I sensed when I was there.
It is that love regardless of if I succeed or fail.
A fathering of sorts. A father I have yet to be,
But I believe
That winning is yours already.
Not from what you have done,
But from who you are in the world.

So, you may not even listen to me,
But one day you will look back and surely see
That this was just another day…
You are still a winner in my book anyway.

Control You No More

If I ever told you anything
Remember this: you do not need me
Or anyone.

If I ever had a job
Or a task as far as you and I
It would be to set you free

Free from burdens
Free from fear
Free from doubt
Free to be who you desire to be

Understand

I visited the harbor today
On the island
Where the sailboats were
Setting out for a day on the sea.
I thought about what you used to say
About sailing and ships,
And everything we never did,
Everything you knew absolutely nothing about.
I guess I knew nothing about sailing either.

But when, in the early morning,
I saw one start to sail away from the docks
Carried strong by the wind and moving away
From me where I stand
And never looking back,
It made me believe I will see you again
When my ship gets carried away by the wind
And I sail away one day too.

Your ship has sailed,
And you knew it would one day
You said so.
But I believe I will see you again
One day,
Even if I remember our days forever together.
I understand, you had to go, for now.

Let it Fly

If I could be thankful,
And content where I live,
I would.
And I would only venture out
Beyond these tame walls,
These comfortable surroundings
To somewhere I could grow, expand, extend my wings.
I feel some days I am surrounded by so many so close to death,
In age and years that is.
One day I will be there too,
I can never return to youth.
But I am so inspired by sound from this younger generation.
Breathes of hope, wonder, conquering.
I am not quite a millennial, but I love the City of Dreams.
And I love the blinding lights of the Entertainment Capital of the world.
Love.
And one day I just might leave these confining walls,
For somewhere like these two cities.
Comfort could be deceiving here in the suburbs of America.
What if this is all I can do?
What if this is everywhere I will ever go?
What if my hometown spits me out and I can't seem to break free?
Can't seem to move on?
Some of my friends from the older days should read some of this stuff.
They may not recognize me, they may wonder where I am today.
One day, I will be free, entirely. Free from continuous striving toward
    getting ahead.
Free from competition completely.
Free from trying. Free from being left behind, and completely abandoned.
Will the money solve everything?
Everybody perks up when the topic is approached.
I love luxury just like anyone, but what would happen then?
Would I have enemies?
I seek to only make peace if possible
While I let it all go…
While I try
To let it fly.

Not Too Late

It is after midnight, far into the early morning hours.
Not a soul is around, no cars on the road, and only the cold outside.
So much I want to say, so much I should tell the world,
Leave something for when I am gone…
But I feel like I have little left to say…
Little left to say to anyone.
Like I am unable to speak so fast and be excited in chatter.
So, I listen more, instead of making sound.
I actually listen to the quiet of the night, the peace.
I am resting, yet not asleep. I am listening, yet there is little sound.
If there is ever a moment to forgive, now is the time.
If there is ever a time to trust, now is the time.
Restoration is on the way.

Hello

All I want is to be known, all I have is the hours in a day.
All I need is air and water, and maybe a little adventure along the way.
I do not need a lot, not many, or to be known by the masses.
Just known by a few, someone I pass along the way, another life just
wanting to say hello.
I think I ran into you today.
Or was it you who found me?
I was all bundled up for the weather outside…you walked over, unexpectedly.
It felt good to see you, you must have been on a holiday or a travel trip.
You were ecstatic, happy, and cracked a smile.
The sun rose, and the crisp air felt cleaner.
The clouds began to break and the burdens I carried that day began to lift.
For whatever reason, I could return home now knowing everything will
be alright.
Some days I start to think I am too old for these moments.
Some days my physical body groans and I sense my time passing too
quickly on the earth.
But not this day.
I am young again, I am light as a feather, and I see clearly once more.
I am sure I will see you again.

Wonder

Here I go at it again
Getting the heck out.
Flying from the airport to somewhere happier…
A place where I can be myself again
A place where I can live a little and see again.
I get this feeling like I wonder
If anyone will ever get to hear me.
Like do I need to be famous in order for someone to understand anything
     I write?
Getting jacked up only lasts a short time.
Getting plugged by so many laughing and wondering
What the hell I am doing all this for anyway?

You could ask me about money and how I need it,
But it would only be part of the story.
I wonder, what to live for now?
I do not fear dying, happens to everybody.
These legs of a beautiful woman keep my attention.
These sounds of desperate youth with dreams keep me writing.
And I know I can't stop, from now until the end, until the certainty drops.
Sounds that perk me up, grab my ear, ease my questions, finding me
     drinking. And listening.
And smoking.
And writing and writing and writing.

Tease me until I am broke: I will still be around, joker.
And I will choose to love even more.

Money

Bored here, bored today, alone.
Few respond even to a text.
Like the whole world has dropped away,
Or at least away from where I am.
No matter what their age, they look away.

Maybe it has to do with money.
Most things seem to come down to money.
Old age and church and just steal it from them.
Like every conversation it seems.
Like every person wants to talk about money with everyone,
Except me.

Bugatti, Ferrari, where is yours?
So clean, so pure, so fast.
But you worked so hard for that,
You deserve it.
I love cars.
Especially fast ones.
Until I can learn to park straight
I will hope to drive the cheapest sports car made.
Until I burn it out, or it breaks down.
And I have to settle for something better.

The Review

They are combing through your text, man, your script.
Every word, every comma, every sentence and period.
Like: for real, it is going through the process.
No feedback, only updates.
No responses or critics, only updates.

I get inspired to write through the music scene, through clubs and the art
   deco.
But tonight, it seems too dangerous to go down there, to the club.
Too many fights, police, racial wars, and the music was just too fast last
   time.
So, I guess I just stay here, on an island, for tonight.

I can go easy, be easy for a little while, as long as I can still express these
   words.

River City Swag

It was a night like tonight, with the moon over the bright lights…
Not exactly the city of brotherly love,
But love was still in the air.
I was young, or younger than I am today.
I thought my town was everything.
I thought I had arrived.
Then I heard something from another level.
A sound like no other hurled through the air to my eardrums.
The beat, the bass, the tone moved my soul.
I heard nothing else, thought of nothing else for a few minutes
Except for the sound of the beat.
Call it mesmerized, entranced, numbed to the world around me.
Those moments are always here and gone,
Like the days of youth and like my opportunity to express this.

Even though I am so much older than that night,
I still maintain a little peace from the sound and the light.
Visually, I saw some woman in a tight dress standing in line to pay a cover
    at the door.
Despite the security guards, despite the Metro providing a sense of calm,
I felt upended. I felt like I could not stay.
But I so remember to this day, the sound from the music played so loud.
I can only hope to carry that night with me forever…
Everything from the clarity, the crispness of the air, the smell of somebody's
    intoxicating perfume,
And even the crowd standing by.
But where was I?
I was walking in the city of never goodbyes.
The place I grew up, the place so familiar, the town I once believed in.
How I so dream of being there again.
Until that day, I will be on my way, creating more words for the few who
    might follow,
And for the ones I left behind.

Create

My body is aging
Bones are aching
Muscles sore from lack of use and stiffness.
The time slips away, and love translates into a few extra pounds at the
 waist.
I know, I know, do not remind me: I am not 21 any longer.
But a new attitude has emerged: embracing the passage of time.
No regrets, no lack of purpose anymore.
No "wish we could re-live the old days" anymore.
Those days are long gone.
Memories I carry: some great, some withered.
Nowadays, all I could use is a response or two, a phone call, or a text
 from a loved one.
If there was one.
So, if all I can do is create…
If all I can be is mundane and quiet and reflective,
I will choose to expand my views, my perception of stuck.
I will need to work harder, and I will need to let love embrace me where I
 am.
I should not need more recklessness, haphazard randomness,
 meaninglessness, waste.
I would reside in love's ocean, in the waters of redemption, in the all-
 agreeing arms of hope.
For now, I will choose to be shielded from quarrels and debate, from
 arguments and hate.
For now, I will choose to only create, and live a wild existence all day
 long.

Closer

I would be closer to you if you opened up a little.
I would be better if you would forgive me a little.
Not in every way, and not every day.
But in one or two ways.
Just a little every now and then.
Like a light in the night, like a ray from a reflection of the sun.
Just a little.
Not a lot, not even more than a few seconds.
Not even feeling an emotion or a tear,
Just a relaxation, just a rest
From anger, from fear, from pointing the blame, or trying to win.

You win.

Trust is something that is earned, not guaranteed.
It often takes a while, at least it does for me.
It is not that we could not,
It is that I could not.
Control me no more, and ask me to do nothing.
But just stay a little closer, stay awake, stay alive, and stay well.

You will see more of me, I am sure.
Through anything, and through everything we can make it.
You make me a better person.

Cold Foundation

The wood floor in my house
Is not real wood. Looks like it, but it's not real.
Could have fooled me.
There were even instructions on how to take care of it…
Mostly what not to do.
Not what is possible, possible with fake wood floors.
I had a choice. I could have selected real wood.
Could have had shiny oak floors, maybe alder in the halls.
To no avail, it is not going to change any time soon
Because it is all down and sturdy.
I walk on this floor every day,
It takes its beating of wear and tear.
It sure is holding up well, after everything,
After all the trampling
And stampedes.
After all the hurried days
Of not even realizing the floors are good-looking.
It was never my doing,
Never my design, never my work.
Only a specialist made it, installed it, took care of it, and showed me how
    to care for it.
A real floor; oh, it is real.
One thing I have not done: slept on this hard floor.
If it was truly wood, it would likely be harder and colder than the current
    type.
But I guess I could rip it all out, put down the real thing, improve the
    overall type.
But it would not change much,
Not of how I use it.
It supports me, after all.
It is something to stand on,
Something to bear upon.
It is directly on top of the foundation of my house.
My house sits on solid gray concrete: talk about cold.
How long will this home last,
How long will the foundation hold up?
If it is a good one, it should last my lifetime,

Or even longer, despite the neighborhood.
But what would make me move off of this foundation?
Would a different one be a better one?
Moving is always stressful,
And I am tired of moving. But what about a real foundation?
A real wood floor?
Does it even matter?
I can be content; I promise I can.
At least for a while.

Feeling Blue

Heavy, over-stressed, humid, and hot day.
There is not a soul to consult.
Maybe a text or a smile near the coffee stand,
Or just silence.
Peace is not bad, but today, the silence is broken with doubt about the
    future.
How will this situation pan out? How will I get through this?
Man, I am so stressed about this.

I must get a grip on a balance.
A balance with what I do, where I go, who I say hello to.
Generosity can go both ways,
If I am not drunk, and I am sincere.
But what about the heat today and in here?
I cannot put more energy toward this, I feel like I will struggle to move on.
But everything does go on, eventually.
They say time heals all things,
Man, I am so needing this.

Give it some hours, let it go, fade away.
I am so needing this.
One day, I will fully be rid of such feelings of blue and humid.
Certainty will catch up to me, and I shall never be afraid of certainty.

For the Time is Short, the Time is Now

There must be a greater good.
There must be agreement.
Fighting cannot be sustained; it is too costly.
There must be a rest and a way to be at ease, at peace.
With all the debating, and all the competing,
What happens to generosity and the golden rule?
With all the time zones, currencies, and deadlines,
What happens to our communication?
Seriously, is it shoved into a schedule, a policy, or a planner?
If time were no issue, and you were not so driven for wealth,
What would you do with your day?
If someone released you from the hustle and the strain of the pay,
How would you respond, how would you use your days on the earth?
When I see the earth and all the people everywhere scattered throughout
I believe we were meant to live together, helping each other, sharing our
stories
By the firelight.
Is it always just a quest to build your name and your legacy?
Nothing wrong with being a philanthropist, I have benefitted you should
know.
Do you want to be remembered?
Do you want to improve the world?
Do you want to shield natural resources and preserve the global
environment?
The outdoors are grand, from the mountains to the canyons to the rivers
and oceans.
I only hope that my actions during my time on earth be filled with respect
and honor.
Respect for life and respect for the earth.
Honor for truth and sacrifice conducted on my behalf.
I concluded: does my time on earth really need to be so hard, such a strain,
so tough?
It is a quest to find the time, and to pen the right words, even to a stranger.
But I hope to speak to more than just my own,
At least as long as I can.

Greater

Greater is everything than just what is seen.
Bigger is the world, more than I can understand.
Larger are the oceans, languages are spread across the distance.
Beyond is everything that cannot be seen or experienced.
But we know with certainty, there is so much more.

Some days I wander back to the suburbs and the sprawl,
Away from the big city and the lights,
And I am still.
Quiet just enough to look up
Into the night sky.
I can see little other than
Billions of tiny dots we are supposed to think are other suns and stars.
How little we really know,
How bored we get with each other here,
And how much we could realize
If occasionally one looked upward into the night.

Guess the stellar professionals know all about these other suns.
Guess the information is out there,
But even the internet with all the data is
Confined to the globe, to the earth, to the visible world.

But I can still feel good, still laugh for a good reason, and still have a little
    fun here on the earth,
Where everything we know is so finite.
There is more, more than we know, a greater space to enter into one day.

Hear It, Find it, Discover More

Music and art have kept me company recently.
Certain music, not everything.

A sound from Los Angeles or something new.
A slower beat and rhythm, a rhyme, a tune to hum to.
It is really the one thing, the only thing, that helps me through some days.
Call it a relative, call it a companion, but I guess it is what the art form does
For many, I realize.

There is a sound of welcome, expression, and acceptance,
A confidence that things are ok, for this song, at least for now.
A mere feeling from music comes and goes, I won't try to capture it
I cannot try to define or explain it, or can I?
Only share it out there every once in a while
At least the sounds that impact me, the ones that really help me.

It is usually the type of sound that is full of talent, yet sounds smooth and
little slower
Along with sounding on key and melodious.
Words affect the sound of the tune, but the music gives words a new place
in the air,
A brand-new form of relating to others.

Not everyone really loves music like I do.
Not everyone will hear the same thing in the same tune,
Especially if there is age difference.
But that is exactly what music does, it breaks down differences and norms,
Traditions and posturing rules.

Some sounds will last a few months or years, others will last decades.
There is a certain impression I get when I hear the name of a famous
composer
From centuries ago.
It is classic and traditional, yet it is very famous, I guess.
Like a sound that is still used in commercials and product advertisements.
But the sound is never new.

There is a lifetime quest for hearing newness, youth, creation of new art,
    and sound.
Youth fades, as does a lot of new music.
Some older songs serve as inspiration for newer artistic expression.

My experience has led me to travel, and to let the newer music take a home
In a place where I might go.
In a way, the sound tends to find me, or I discover it,
Or something like that.
It is always a rush, to uncover something I have never heard before.
Something that helps me through, interprets in many ways,
Aligns the world to the way it should be
Even for just a few minutes.

Possible

If it were possible to stay here, I would
If it were possible to rest here, I could
If it be possible to smile here, I should
But I am moving on, from here.

If I felt a little peace here, I would stay
If I sensed a little potential here, I would dive in
But I am still digging in
And I probably need to find something soon

For all I have is time and hours and days
To spend the right way
On expression and on relation
To one who might listen

I am not a wanderer, more of a solo trekker
I do not climb mountains anymore
Though I did once
Call me an old friend

There was youth once,
Gone in a moment and I was old
But still moving and rocking in the wind
Like a post from a sailboat with a few nautical miles logged in

I will not try to sound super intelligent
I will not be fake or nonchalant
I will say the truth, what you might understand
I will relay what might be possible in the end.

Miles

Mr. Miles, if it is alright to say so,
I believe I owe you some gratitude, a debt I could not repay.
You see, you pushed me over the edge,
Over my fear and over my expectations of who I was,
And who I could be.
Mr. Miles, if it is ok, could you just slow down and listen for a minute.
I promise, I will not be long, I promise.

I want you to know:
I stopped talking.
I started listening, listening to artists.
And I started writing.
Really, really writing. For real.

Remember that one day when I was hesitant,
When I could not figure out what to do
For the life of me,
When it had to do with her,
You told me to cut out the bull.
That was so true, and so right.
You would never believe it now, but that night, my life changed.
For the good, you know?
So much changed for me that night with her,
And I have no clear vision for where you are today,
But I hope it is in a good place.
I hope you "made it", in every sense of the phrase.

Still, Mr. Miles, without your words, without your voice and concern,
I might still be so stuck.
In a way, you were there for a reason, somehow by chance.
But all I can express, if you would let me, Mr. Miles,
Is my thanks, and my expression of the long-term results of your words
    and care.
Honestly, it has been so many years I forget what you even look like,
Other than maybe a shaved or bald head and a fierce face.
We were so young then, and in a way, we still are.
If you would realize, Mr. Miles, what happened inside my soul that night.

Vagueness and ambiguity have a way of interpretation over time.
You definitely held zero haze, zero mirky words, and zero mincing of
    words.
I needed it, and I am grateful.

I finally found out how I am wired,
I finally found out how I am made.
It is not always making me billions,
But I have a roadway,
A path, an aim, a direction.
And I am so grateful.

That is all Mr. Miles.
You are free to go now.
Just as you helped me to be so many years ago.
I remember you today, and you know more than me
That you are completely and totally free.

Hold on to What You Love

Now is the day and time,
Now is the most important day of your life.
Weak and tired you might be feeling,
Like a horse who has traveled many roads and needs rest.
From always running and going,
From being jerked and steered.

"But I must work, I need a purpose" you say.
True, everyone needs to work.
But now is all you have, now is all there is.
If you love something, chase it, go after it, find it, do it.
Many days spent doing nothing at all.
But if you love doing nothing at all, it's ok too,
For a while.
Rest is needed, I know, I hear you saying it loud.

Conclusion: do not waste.
Do not let go of what you love.
Find it, or let it find you.
But master it, spend time there.
For there you will feel alive,
And there you might always return.
At least as long as there is something to return to.

My House

My house is so simple, nothing real fine or fancy.
It is truly all I need; it is just me hiding in this place.
Gets quiet a lot, but I keep it going.
It is only a few years old.
I found the site a few years back.
They took a while to put it all together, the builders,
Roof and all.
It is only a building, nothing to get excited about.
They colored it grey; the inside is bright
With wood floors and dark furniture.
I like it.
It could use a woman's touch,
But then it would be mostly her's. It would cease to be my house.

No one really works around here, mostly retired folks and healthcare
    workers.
I am not a doctor, not a medical person, but I like the street.
It is so quiet, especially on Sundays.
During the week, they spend most days building and constructing the
    homes
Behind us.
But its ok, the traffic ceases
After around six.

Some days, I wish I had at least a swimming pool, or a place to host a pool
    party.
Even though the beach is only
Twenty minutes or less.
But all I ever wanted was peace and quiet for a home.
Would still have room for a happy hour
After hours one night,
When the time is right.
And you do not need to remind me,
I am bringing the wine.
My house is slowly, even timidly becoming a home.
I am so grateful.

Our Town

Where you live, I may never go.
Where you work, I may never see.
Where you play, I might only hear about,
But the town is yours.

You may not own everything in sight,
You may not own anything at all.
And you may have arguments in your town,
But the town is yours.

A place brings a part of who you are,
Something more than just a time period on earth.

The more I listen, the more I read, the more I believe
That you, like me, are made to relate somehow.
It might be through a book or a tune,
But somehow, I could hear about the place
You call home too.

Some may move all over the globe.
Some may never settle for anything close
To a town of origin.
But where you are could be all you are.

I guess that is where I come from: a town.
This town happens to be part of a city,
And the city is part of a country.
All else aside, and no matter how much I want to move away,
It will always be a part of me, and I a part of it
For a time, for a while.

If your town kicks you out, find a place to call your town.
In my book, towns are not ranked in value.
All are part of a greater existence called humanity,
Where we are free to live in safety, and where we are suited to be
From a place we call our town.

*End note: for musical parallel, inspiration, and smiles, listen to "Our House" by Madness.

Today

Quiet, not a sound in the house.
Birds outside and a shower of rain
Cooling off the summer heat.

Today is a Sunday.
No one calls, not even to say hello
Or to check in, as if they cared.
But neighbors up early and walking before the rain.

Today is nearly half spent. Time is the currency.
I have much less of it now than I did this morning.
Tomorrow will bring enough cares and the week will start to grind out
Like tires of a fire engine
Creating friction
With the summer roadways.
But not today.

Quiet, all is still. I have no idea where everyone is.
Might be the beach, might be sleeping, who knows.

I wish I could say
I had a family today, to be with, to chat with.
But I am all grown up and we have diverged so much,
At least in location.
A text is great, but that is all it ever seems to be nowadays.
Social media has its perks, if everyone in the family hops onto the trend
And sports a new post every now and then.

Between knapping and wondering,
I remain at peace
Only for today.
The grind will have its way,
But not today, not today.

I awoke early this morning
To the steam and the fog from the sprinklers on the lawn.
Awoke wondering about those who I knew well, and those who are now
     gone.
Not gone forever, yet sad to miss them from this life.

I awoke today
To video sounds of cheering crowds, sounds of victory, and motivational
     speeches
Of inspiration and of hope.
One day, I will join the victors who have won their final race,
Who are no longer with us here, but only in our hearts and minds, and I
     might still see their face,
But not today.
Today is a gift, today, today.

Falling

I fell for you, hard.
It was more than just a crush.
Maybe it was how you spoke, maybe it was your body.
I really had no idea what the hell happened.
It happened so fast, and I was so sure I knew what I was doing.
Until the ground beneath my feet crumbled and I shuttered.
You gave me more than just a second chance, and I still feel so bad
About the way I behaved.
I cannot stop remembering how we were together, like a miracle.
Like my heart was too weak, or too frail, and you sustained it.
And when you have something great, you do not want to lose it, or ruin it.
But I did. I guess I did. I guess it was me, not you.
I guess.
But so many years have gone by, and we drifted away into the greyness of
    age.
I was so young back then, and I should have known better, but I fell, fell
    hard.
From now on, I will always remember the good days, the little bit of thrill,
With yet another woman who might know a little more about me than
    she should.

Saying Goodbye

I guess it is goodbye; goodbye for now.
From the inside out, my energy is drained.
Every emotion has been spent. Every tear exited my eyes.
I never thought I would feel this way, this tired and exhaustive sense of
    loss.
You loved me so well, and now you are gone forever.
It might take me a few days, months, or years.
But we have so many happy memories, so many great times together.
You lived a great life, yet it felt cut short for tough reasons I do not fully
    understand.
I guess your time came, you hopped on the last train home.
And I believe that is where you rest now: home.

With all my words poured out, nothing will bring you back.
But I will always hope
And pray that others will be blessed and found through your life well-lived.
You worked so hard, set great goals, and became so successful
In my eyes.
I am glad I was able to relay how proud I was of you,
Even though I did not know
Those would be the last words I would ever get to say to you.

We scattered your ashes at sea today, early at sunrise.
This was your last and final wish, and we carried out your orders.
And as the wind blew over the Atlantic Ocean, and as the sun began to
    beautify
And highlight the place you spent so much time
With orange and purple and blue light piercing the clouds over the horizon,
I stood in the warm surf as your ashes graced the water and wind.
You are no longer here, and I will miss you so much.
You joined the great adventure of the afterlife.
And I believe one day I will meet you again in that great adventure,
Where there will be newness, joy again, and we will fully understand,
And I will no longer need to say goodbye.

It Matters

Does it really matter?
Does it really matter where I live?
Does it matter if I am showered and shaven?
Really, what matters?

Does it matter if I do not work out?
Does it matter if I eat too much?
Does it matter if no one wants to chat it up?
Really, I guess I am wondering myself.

No time to waste, no time but today.
I know, I know…
You are so smart.
It is only that feeling of love that keeps me going.

That love thing sneaks up on me
Like a magic opening of a new hotel.
Like a runway for a Victoria's Secret model in Milan.
That love keeps me going.

So, listen: tell it to me straight.
I am going to be here, stay here for now,
For this year. Next year, it
Might be a whole new story.

Forgiving

The best days are ahead.
Aging and grey-haired days.
Being in Florida these people are everywhere
And from everywhere.
New York, California, Syria, everywhere.
All of these people have lived such amazing days.
Their age
Holds with it experience and insight,
For those
Who will take the time.
Turn down the noise for them
And listen to them.
They would listen to you again and again
If only you would let them in.
I know they are from another time,
Another generation, another moment so different.
But they need us.
They need our voice.
They need our listening.
And they matter.
They are such lives of greatness,
These with grey hairs.
So, I look up to them,
Not for their ability to understand everything
About the younger folks,
But for giving them some of my time.
For giving, and forgiving.
It is a give and take: give a little, receive a little.
Because who knows, one day
I might be their age.
And it will happen so soon.
I look forward to these future days.

Wild Blue

When I wander outside of this house…
When I venture beyond these four walls
When I explore…
There is so much to view
Under the great wild blue
Skies above.
The canopy that covers the earth,
Separates the heavenly space from the atmosphere
Even with the days
Of cloud cover.

If I were to travel above it all
I would be able to view
Everything under the great wild blue.

There is nothing to fear
Except for the rain that might ruin our plans
To explore and venture outdoors.
But I will go anyway, out in the rain.
It is all a part of the dome, a part of the world.
Natural.

There one day might be more details
About the ways to explore
Beyond our planet's doors
And through the rest of this place
We call space.

When I look up at night,
When the blue skies have vanished for the evening
And the sun begins to set,
I see how big this space is.

So much I do not know,
So much to one day explore,
So much and with a feeling of wonder:
What else would there be to see?

Beyond these colors of light
There is more.
There is so much more to see.
Until then I will choose to love and dwell in my home anew
Under the cover of the vast wild blue.

Physicality

I wish I could tell you I always feel fearless.
I wish I could shake off every physical sickness, virus, ailment.
With no one's help.
I wish I was never aging and never growing old.
But I feel it beginning, even now.
I guess I have always felt it.
The physical changes that occur as a result.
The increased stiffness,
The occasional lack of energy,
Call it a virus, call it a sickness, this human frailty.
Of course, there are other days when risk is everything,
Throw reason to the wind, and settle on an experience by chance.
I once believed my youth would last forever, at least internally.
But when I run into those who have surpassed me in age
In the market, on the street,
They seem so aware, so astute, and so kind.
Slower they usually walk, and they notice everyone
Even if they never say hi, and even if I do not know them.
But they always see me,
And I always see them.
And I wonder.
Will I live to be their age?
What will I think at that age?
What condition will I be in?
Will I look back more, or look forward more?
At age forty-one, I find it tough to look back
Even a little bit. My memory fails me often.
And I tend to hear and see the here and now.
So that is where I remain: one day
At a time. Just living one day
At a time.

On Success

Where I once believed I had won,
Where I held confidence and joy,
Where I found admiration,
I now see it only as part of the big picture.
A piece of the greater story told.
A fragment of the pinnacle of my life.
Professional wins, economic status, peer respect,
All of this is part of success.
But only a part.
Real success is who I truly loved in my life,
And who truly loved me in return.
I feel it now: their success. In a way, their success
Is now part of my success.
Maybe not precisely in how I have worked, nor
How definitely I have accomplished anything,
But in their love for me.
That is my biggest reward: to be loved.
Truly, imperfectly, and victoriously loved.
I turn it around and begin to wonder: who do I truly love?
For those who I can,
For the few who I have received much love from,
If I can count those days, those moments with them,
I would add up the time to measure success.
The moments that really matter, the moments you remember,
And the moments you wish would live forever.

Fighting Boredom

There is no way to explain it.
There is no way around it.
If you are just plain bored,
There is nothing but time and to wait it out.
Days pass when boredom never relates to me.
There are other days I cannot wait to move on to the next
Day.
Some minutes of boredom seem to last forever.
But there, in the slowness, in the delay of all things, I am challenged
To not just endure,
But to enjoy…
Enjoy my time for this life is so short.
I refocus and redetermine how to spend my time more efficiently.
And the boredom subsides, at least for a while.
But knowing no boredom is to never speak of endurance.
My indulgence in a book always paves the way
To better hours of the day.
After which I can finally smile again.
And put behind me minutes that feel wasted.
They are never wasted, never, but it feels like that.
To rise above, to learn from my mistakes, and to emerge
Lighter: my hope.
And I believe there is always hope,
Always.

It Was History

There might be a time, when all will be understood.
There might be a day, when I will fully comprehend
The days that seemed meaningless and long.
When I remember the grand times, the parties, the weddings, the concerts
I will remember you.
Because you were there through it all.
In the ups and the downs
No matter how many ways I might express it.

There might be a day when I feel so much better
Then how I felt when we were together.
Even for such a short time
You and I were a blaze.
I will remember those days.
The days set the pace
For me and for my ways
Of trying to relate
Or at least the hope of the real thing.

You must understand, I have a very low tolerance
For anything but the real and for love.
It is how I may be wired.

She would not provide more.
And it was over. Over for then, over forever.
It was my first taste of love.
And I wanted so much more.

Today I Fear Nothing

For our time together,
For what we made together,
Forever
I am still around here;
Whole-heartedly,
And I find myself stronger
And fearing nothing
Because of our love.

The business world can eat you up
It's all about the money man, for real.
Everything.
For real, until it all is enough to make you crazy.
Everyone wants to live comfortably
To get what you need.
But our time together was beyond the working world.
You helped me remember where I came from,
Maybe even how I was made, and why.
I was not made perfect, but never out of fear.

It was never about what we should do.
It was never about what we were made to do.
It was what we wanted. What you wanted. No arguing.
But maybe the day will be around that we feel like we must argue
For some damn reason
To matter
To someone again, but I will never forget
How you helped me not to fear, anything anymore.

You opened me up. It was more than me.
It was us.

Nothing but the Same

Nothing.
Nothingness.
Forever, here in this big town.
Everyone leads the same life.
It's what you are supposed to do, what you are expected to do.
I wish I could live the life you lived, man.

All jacked up, on everything but the truth.
Starting with no excuse,
Of where I should go.

But at the end of my life
I want there to be no excuse
Of where I went
Or what happened to me.
In simplicity
From here to there
I lived.
That is what I want others to believe.

Not in some faraway fantasy,
Or in an unknown mystery,
But it was my time, my life.
There was never a day I doubted,
That my life was a gift.
That life is a gift, a sacred memory to cherish.
From me to you, this day, be real, and follow the truth
Until you can never be bored anymore.
From here to there, I believe.

I Wish I Could

I wish I could go where you want me to go.
It is not that I am fighting it.
It is not that I do not think there is good there.
But are these people really happy there?
Or do they wish and hope and not think anything better could become
    of them?

Singing off-key, out of tune, every week, does something to me.
I wish I could, I wish I could see what you see, hear what you hear,
Love what you love, go where you go, understand why you stay there.
But I move on.

But these words will never reveal
How thankful I am for you
And all the time you spent on my growth
And I will never forget you.

Never Looking Back

Real: time ticks away.
Ever so slowly
Some days.
Not growing any younger.
Can't go back.
Can only go forward.
Yes, I'm alright.

Won't analyze,
Won't overreact,
But I will express
These concerns about my lifetime
Am I living it right?
I guess no one knows.

In the end, I grow closer and closer to old age.
41 right now, more than halfway
To 80.
But really, what is it like
To make it to 80?
Wow, will I be happy
When I am old?
When all I do is wish I were young again.

I guess no one will ever see
How I will never look back
In envy
Or for anything.
One way forward.
I think of it as certainty.

Hear It

There is a rhythm.
Breaking all the rules.
Free and uncontaminated.
When I hear it for the first time
And when I see you sing it
It makes me free.
I can't explain why.
I don't know why.

Express yourself, keep going, let it all out.
Free.
Create, be free, and unwind.
Spread the love, let me grab a scotch.

So many are scared these days.
So many feel locked in their houses.
So many feel so bored and chained up.
God help us.
Be free.
Be you. Only you.
And make a little cash on the side
So we could meet in Vegas.
In a five-star hotel or maybe Caesar's Palace.
Either way, be you, no one else.
You know I cannot go without ya.

You Make it a Night to Remember

There was a time when I never knew who you were.
There was a time when we never held each other close.
How I forgot those days, they are long gone.
Over, like the end of a show or a movie worth the wait.
But with you here and now, the scent of your perfume,
The way your body moves
It makes me feel so loved.
I am so glad you found me again.
I wish you would stay with me tonight longer and forever.
It might just be a feeling or a passing notion,
But it never seemed so real.
You make me better. You make me smile. You keep me honest.
And you make it worth every minute.
I have never felt this way before.

All Will Work Out

Love
In the middle of the grime and the mess
In the center of a world under duress
In a town aged and unhealthy
In a place way too unsanitary
Rotten
Deteriorating
Needing maintenance and so much more.
Love
In the place where it is hard and difficult
In the way that I can
No matter how uneasy I believe
The time is short.
My dream is only to matter.
But my time is short.
I wrestle with how to spend my life
And I sometimes doubt everything
Will be ok.
But it's through inspiration that I accept the wings to let my fear go.
It's through others that I feel a purpose.
Looking inside lasts only until you can share and express.
Somehow, all will work out.
Some way, all will work out.
Somehow, everything will be ok.

Our Time

I woke up one day, a morning with much new sunlight.
I realized my age, and that I am never getting younger,
Only older and not going back.
How do I act my age?
I love this newer music, but it always seems to emerge from a youthful
artist.
It still makes me want to drink and dance, but one day I might be too old.
Youth fades yet is so popular to cling to.
My only hope is that my time left will become "our time".
My fear is spending so many remaining hours by myself.
I admit, I am so independent.
But our time is not my time. It does not belong to me anymore.
It belongs to us.
That is where I will be content, that is where I might relax.
Together,
Sharing thoughts and hopes and wonders of the world.
This is why I vacation so much; this is why I love the newer music and
such.
It is shared, it is transcendent of just me, alone.
It brings me connected to you, and it begs me never to leave again.

Big Beer Tummy

This is not the first time,
And I am sure it will not be the last.
This is definitely not the first one
And one day I will need to pass
On ordering another.
It is not even beer I love,
But the growth of the body indicated a change,
An unwanted noted change.
Drastic.
Take me to the gym, run me down the sidewalk,
Anything you want me to do or say
To make this go away.
But there is little hope
Unless I start to drink less
And then confess
My extended stomach was never intentional.
It might have occurred as a result of a party or two.
It may have resulted from lazy bones.
But I know this: it is real, it is present.
And I should reduce it.
If I have the means.
Because I only get older, not younger.
But it is so hard
To change some days.
So tough.